Clone 71: The Brotherhood

I0666840

By Matthew Reade

First Edition
Printed in the United States

ISBN: 978-0-6151-9319-9

This book is dedicated to Mateo, to thank him for hatching this dream, and to Janice, my grandmother, for her generous support of my writing.

Preface

Have you ever had or heard of a dream that gave you an idea? Well, that's how I came to write this book.

One of my friends, Mateo, told me about a dream he had had the night before.

His dream was about a clone that was imprisoned in a facility deep underground. He finally got the sense to escape the wretched place with a few of his brethren after getting a whiff of what the cloners were going to do.

I was obviously amazed by the detail and quality of this dream, so I urged him to go on.

So, in front of my eyes, Mateo weaved an amazing story about clones, war, and treason. And so this book was born.

Enjoy!

Table of Contents

Chapter 1
Normal Life

A man rolled out of his bed and fell onto the hard metal floor, bumping his head. The man swiftly got up and swore harshly before walking into the bathroom to take a shower.

This man was Clone #71, one of the first clones made by the two down on luck cloner twins, James and Michael Schwartz. The cloners had built the huge underground facility for many reasons, all of them unknown.

This particular clone looked exactly like Michael Schwartz. He was handsome, yet muscular, and was quite thin for his build.

Clone 71 finished showering and dressed in his guard clothes; white shirt and pants with leg and chest armor. He put his red security key into his pocket and slipped out of the door to his room, ignoring his roommate's snores.

The clone walked down the marble halls, occasionally looking out the clear bulletproof windows to correct his direction. Finally, after a while, he turned and hurried up a flight of stairs to enter a large intersection where several hallways met. He then sidled over to the entrance to the largest hallway and stood guard there.

After a while, Clone 71 was joined by two other guards, who nodded in his direction and stood again, stiff as boards.

Suddenly, an explosion rocked the facility. Clone 71 was thrown to the ground hard as dark gray smoke filled the air. Coughing, he stood up and ran into the smoke, following the sound of someone running ahead.

Clone 71 fell on his back again to avoid a hissing rocket shell that slammed into the wall next to him. He flew into the air, smashed into the opposite window, and crumpled to the floor. The clone then drew out his laser pistol and fired five times down the corridor. He waited for a few seconds, listening for a cry or yelp that would signify a hit. He heard nothing, so he got up and ran down the corridor again.

Finally, the smoke dissipated. Clone 71 immediately spotted his quarry running a few feet in front of him. He grinned and fired his pistol. Or tried to. The barrel wasn't working!

He then looked at the two-person tram ahead and got a crazy idea.

He chased the man to the tram. The man jumped inside, locked it, and started the engine.

Just as the tram left the docking port, Clone 71 jumped onto the back of it and hung on.

The ride up the clear tram tubes was difficult. Clone 71 tried not to think about what would happen if he lost his grip and tumbled down the vertical tube to his death.

Finally, he made his move. He climbed slowly to the bottom of the tram and sighed. "I'm glad these float," thought the clone. "Honestly, this is madness."

He held on to a bar as he dug in his pocket for an ice pack. He found one and tied it onto the energy circulation pipe. He then waited.

"I thought this was supposed to wor…"

The engine, under stress from converting freezing biofuels to energy, ruptured, showering Clone 71 with debris. The clone spat out a mouthful of muck and climbed into the slowing tram through a broken window.

The saboteur gazed at him for a moment, and then said slowly, "I am one of you."

Clone 71 smiled briefly. "Yes. Why did you do that to this place?"

The saboteur rubbed his eyes. "Look, okay, this isn't the best time, but I'll make it quick. The clones are being brainwashed! Michael and James want to take over the world using us. They want us to kill innocent people so they can just become richer. That's why I want to…"

The vehicle suddenly stopped, causing a poison dart to slide off of the dashboard, into the young saboteur's arm. The saboteur grunted in pain, and then slumped over, dead.

Clone 71 stared at him for a moment, and then extricated himself from the vehicle. He then walked out of the tube, into a hallway, and headed back to his room.

Chapter 2
Time to Think

Clone 71 slept badly that night. He tossed and turned, rolled and wriggled. But it seemed that nothing would help him sleep.

Finally, the clone dressed in some simple garments and took a walk.

It was rather cold out here at midnight, with a small breeze, created by windmills that were supercharged for an extremely fast speed so the air would move like wind.

Suddenly, the clone heard a noise in the hall in front of him. He stopped and rolled behind a pair of large, heavy barrels. When the sound was gone, he stood up and crept toward the noise.

As he neared the sound, Clone 71 began to notice that two guards were ahead. He realized that the cloners were in the room behind them, talking.

Once again, Clone 71 got a brilliant idea. He reached into his pocket and pulled out a bottle, a rope, two high-grip suction cups, and a foldable metal pike. Then, he began.

The clone gripped the bottle and slung it right between the two guards, breaking the bottle. A blue mushroom cloud blew out of it, right into the two guard's eyes.
The guards stopped talking and placed their hands over their eyes, yelling, "I can't see! I can't see!"

Clone 71 grinned and dodged between them. He stuck a suction cup into one wall and the other cup into the adjacent wall. Then, he pulled out the pike, drew back the rope, and fired the pike like an arrow at the guards.

Both guards got smacked on the back of the head with the pike. They staggered for a moment, and then fell onto the stone floor.

Clone 71 stole the guards' sub-machine guns and crept to the doorway to hear what the two cloners were saying.

"…soon. We won't get away with cloning an *army*, for Pete's sake, honestly, could you ever be more stupid, brother. Next thing we know you'll be cloning tanks to blow up the universe. Are you *crazy???*" James's voice screamed angrily.

"Brother, the clones are under our control. That is… until they leave this place without us." Michael said soothingly.

James's temper died down a bit. "Well, I've handled that. I turned them all to my side."

"*Our* side, brother."

"Yeah, yeah, yeah, but I could…"

Clone 71 turned away from the door to leave, but a laser pistol kept his head pressed against the door.

"Well, well, well, what have we here?" a man dressed in yellow and red armor was next to the clone. "A clone out late. Oh dear, you're in big trouble. Ha ha ha ha ha ha!" He smashed Clone 71 on the side of his head.

The man's laughter was the last thing the young clone heard before he faded into unconsciousness.

Chapter 3
Figuring It Out

Clone 71 woke up to a colossal headache. He bore it as well as possible, but it still felt like the whole cloning structure suddenly grew legs and jumped on his head.

He tried to stretch his sore limbs, but he was chained to a wall with neutral electricity. Then he looked around to figure out where he was.

"I'm in the dungeon," he thought sadly. "How do I get out of here?"

He heard a door swing open and loud voices yelling. Then, it was silence again. A moment later, stepping out from behind a pillar, was James Schwartz. And from behind him stepped Michael.

"Hey, you. Clone 71." James yelled commandingly.

Clone 71 looked up at him with hatred in his eyes. "Yes?"

James shuddered and looked away.

Michael stepped up. "What were you doing?"

The angry clone raged at Michael. "I was taking a walk! You've got a *problem* with that?"

Michael looked down. "Torture him, then release him later, after we leave," he commanded a soldier. "Do it."

With that, the Schwartz twins left the dungeon and walked back to their quarters.

The soldier that was to torture Clone 71 walked over to the electro-dial and placed his hand on it. He began to turn, but then stopped. "You couldn't bring yourself to torture me," said Clone 71. "Thank you."

The clone-soldier twisted the dial to zero and released him. "That's one order I couldn't follow," the soldier said with a growl.

"Yeah," Clone 71 attempted to restore circulation in his arms and legs. "What's your number?"

14

"Oh, yeah. I'm Clone 13," said the soldier briskly. "And this is Royal Guard Clone 34. We call him RG Clone." He motioned to a young clone wearing black armor.

Clone 71 nodded. "I am Clone 71. Good to see you guys."

RG Clone turned and shook his hand. "Hey, man. I think I saw you yesterday."

Clone 71 grinned. "Maybe you did. Good to see you."

Clone 13 gestured toward the dungeon door. "Let's get out of this place. We need to talk."

The clones walked out of the dungeon and into an elevator. RG Clone drew a golden card out of his breast pocket, placed it into the card slot, and pressed the gold button that suddenly appeared on the wall.

The elevator shot upward toward the roof of the enormous complex. Finally, the elevator stopped. The door opened and RG Clone led them out into a large golden room, and then gestured for Clone 13 and 71 to sit down at the large table at the center of the room.

After everyone had been seated, RG Clone cleared his throat noisily and said simply, "What happened?"

Clone 13 grimaced. "Yeah. We'd like to know, because James and Michael Schwartz don't torture people a lot unless they are bad."

"Really bad," added RG Clone.

"Which you aren't," said Clone 13 helpfully.

"Precisely," said RG Clone.

Clone 71 smiled. "Well, where do I start?"

Clone 71 told them everything, from his talk with the saboteur to what he heard from James and Michael Schwartz.

"From what I've heard, I think that saboteur's worst fears have been confirmed. James and Michael Schwartz are going to take over the world with our brethren," finished Clone 71.

RG Clone and Clone 13 exchanged grim looks.

"Well," said RG Clone, "that saboteur was right. Everything that he told you is completely possible. Taking over the world completely fits Michael and James's personalities."

Clone 13 nodded. "Yeah."

Clone 71 grimaced. "All right," he said, "we need to escape this place. I want you two to get ideas. Meet me at the elevator we came here in at midnight tonight."

RG Clone and Clone 13 nodded agreeably.

"I won't miss it," said RG Clone.

"I'll be there," agreed Clone 13.

"Good," said Clone 71. "We need to get out of this mess. And fast!"

Chapter 4
The Great Escape

Clone 71 didn't sleep at all. When he had arrived at his small quarters, he just sat on his bed, staring at the clock.

Fifteen minutes from midnight, Clone 71 finally got dressed it a light but heavily armored uniform. He grabbed a couple grenades, a laser pistol, and a majestic blaster rifle. Then, without hesitation, he slipped through the door and headed downstairs toward the elevator.

Clone 71 left the stairs and turned left. Up ahead was the elevator, gleaming with a strange light.

Suddenly, a gloved hand came around his neck, choking him. Clone 71 reached forward, and then plunged his elbows back into his choker. The gloved hand became limp, and Clone 71 heard a thump behind him.

The young clone grinned grimly. "Got you good," he said to himself quietly as he continued toward the elevator.

The elevator door opened, and a man wearing gold armor walked out.

"Clone 13," exclaimed Clone 71. "Where's RG Clone?"

Clone 13 gestured, and RG Clone walked out from behind him, wearing of all things, purple armor.

"Whoa, RG Clone," said Clone 71, grinning. "Nice armor."

RG Clone winked. "Thanks, man. All right, let's go up."

The three men piled into the elevator. RG Clone slipped a black passkey out of a pocket and placed it into the card slot on the elevator wall. The elevator began moving up.

"So, what's the plan?" asked Clone 71 eagerly.

RG Clone opened his mouth to answer, but closed it again when the elevator door opened to a darkened corridor.

"Be quiet, or they'll hear us," said Clone 13 softly.

"Who'll hear…" Clone 71 began, but was cut off as red lights went off in the corridor and alarms started to flare.

"Just RUN!" yelled RG Clone.

They all began to run as fast as they could down the passage.

Clone 71 took out his laser pistol and turned to see their enemy.

Hundreds of clones dressed in light battle armor were flying in the air after them using jetpacks. Clone 71 swallowed hard. The jet troopers' main weapon was a giant energy launcher with a barrel the size of his head.

Clone 71 took a few shots with his pistol, blasting a jet trooper's jetpack off and knocking him to the floor. He shot one more in the hand, and then put on an extra spurt of speed.

RG Clone, hearing gunfire, turned his head to the right to see if the other two clones were okay. He saw Clone 13, and craning his neck back, he could see Clone 71 running sluggishly from his exhaustion. RG Clone turned toward Clone 13.

"We gotta fight, 13! He's going down!" yelled the royal guard.

"No!" yelled Clone 13.

"Yes!" screamed back RG Clone. "He's the reason why we can leave this place. Come on!"

The young royal guard turned around and pulled a yellow blaster rifle out of his belt. It expanded from a pistol size to a four-foot long behemoth of a rifle. "Come on!" he repeated.

Clone 13 pulled out a portable energy pike and turned around. "Charge!" he yelled confidently.

RG Clone rolled up next to Clone 71 and guarded him with his seemingly infinite amount of blaster fire.

Clone 13 jumped onto a jet trooper's back and ripped the jetpack off of him. He then put it on and flew up to stab and punch the jet troopers that were attacking them.

In the midst of the battle, Clone 71 managed to pull out the small mine that he had brought.

In doing this, he got another amazing idea.

"Pull back!" yelled Clone 71 frantically.

His two partners stepped back.

Clone 71 threw the mine up at one of the troopers. "FIRE IN THE HOLE!!!" he screamed, diving away as the trooper collided with the wall in an effort to escape the mine.

"BOOM!"

The mine exploded, killing or maiming all of the jet troopers. Clone 13 and RG Clone stood up, coughing and choking on the smoke as Clone 71 became visible.

"Wow," exclaimed RG Clone. "That was awesome!"

"Yeah," said Clone 13. "Okay, let's continue."

The three men had been walking for a while when RG Clone spotted something. "Hey guys," he said. "Look, another elevator!"

Clone 71 grinned. "All right, we need to go up there." He pointed at the top level, which was visible through the glass.

He ran to the elevator, with the two other clones following behind. The door opened, and the three clones walked inside.

RG Clone pressed the "H", and the elevator began to move upward.

"What does "H" mean?" asked Clone 71.

"Hanger," said Clone 13. "We'll be able to leave if we get in there." The door opened. "This way, guys." He pointed straight ahead to a giant grey door.

Suddenly, the door opened, exposing a battalion of clones. Half of the clones were armed with blaster rifles; the other half was armed with laser pistols.

RG Clone muttered softly. "Guys, run to the left corridor. I'll hold them off."

"No!" exclaimed Clone 71. "Run for it. I'll cover you! Go now!"

Clone 71 readied his blaster rifle and fired a deadly hail of shots, injuring several clones and killing one. He then leaped to the left corridor and ran to catch up with his two friends.

One of Clone 71's pursuers came into firing range. Raising his pistol, he let six laser bolts fly from his weapon.

Clone 71 ducked as four laser bolts whizzed over him, narrowly missing his skull. One straggling bolt flew way off target, into the wall, while the final shot flew past Clone 71's right arm. The shot flew forward, straight into Clone 13's thigh.

"Ahhhhhhh!" he screamed in pain. The young clone fell, blood gushing from his wound.

Clone 71 urged himself to move faster. Stopping beside Clone 13, he hauled him up onto his back. Despite the sweat pouring down his body from the effort, Clone 71 only ran faster to save his friend.

Meanwhile, RG Clone sprinted through a steel door and into the hanger. He ran to a plane's cargo hold, looked around, and jumped inside.

Clone 71 ran through the door, following RG Clone's footsteps. He also ran to the cargo hold and hid inside.

RG Clone shut the hold door. "What happened to him?" he asked urgently, pointed to Clone 13 motionless form.

"He got hit," replied Clone 71 gravely, "in the thigh."

RG Clone quickly pulled some bandages and disinfectant out of his pocket. "Help me with this," he said wearily.

That moment the plane started to move. Clone 13 grunted in his unconsciousness and turned over.

RG Clone poured disinfectant on the wound, and Clone 71 placed several bandages to finish dressing the wound.

Suddenly the plane lifted off, but with a great deal of rocking. It cruised out of the hanger, and out of the underground facility.

They had escaped!

Chapter 5
Survival

After a minute of flying, the plane's engine stalled. Clone 71 and RG Clone looked at each other anxiously as the plane began its spiral toward the ground. Clone 71 moved toward the window, but blacked out as the plane finally crashed in the middle of nowhere.

Clone 71 awoke with a bitter taste in his mouth. He spat and got up, swearing heavily. "Now what are we going to do?" he muttered angrily. He strode forward, but tripped and fell on a piece of debris. Uttering a new string of curses, he picked himself up and took stock of their surroundings.

The plane had been completely destroyed. It was hard to believe that he had survived the horrible-looking crash. The only part left of the plane was half of the cargo hold. It had been held together by all of the boxes crammed into it.

Suddenly, Clone 71 was startled by a loud groaning noise. Determined to figure it out, he crouched into the cargo hold.

A man lay on the floor of the cargo hold, covered with blood. The man had purple hair and dark, tanned skin. He looked like a lifeguard, if you subtracted the purple hair, of course.

Clone 71 picked him up and carried him out of the cargo hold into a cool place behind a pile of rocks. He cleaned up the man's wounds the best he could, resisting the man's groans of pain. "It's all right. You'll live. Don't worry," he said with a strain in his voice. "Don't worry."

All of a sudden, the cargo hold started to tremble and move upward. Clone 71 looked beneath the cargo hold and saw a grimacing figure pushing the whole section of the aircraft off a limp young man.

The grimacing figure was RG Clone.

Clone 71 left the man's side and ran to help, rolling it over and off the two young men. Finally, after a great deal of effort, the hold finally gave way and shifted away from the two men.

RG Clone fell to the ground, exhausted from the effort. Clone 71 slung the limp young man and RG Clone onto his back and put them down next to the man he had been caring for.

Suddenly, a hand pressed over his mouth and nose, smothering him. Clone 71 pulled the hand off his face, turned, and punched the man who had snuck upon him.

The man fell to the ground, swearing, and then got up slowly. "Sorry about that," he said gruffly. "Didn't know you were a friend."

Clone 71 rubbed his hands together. "It's okay, friend," he muttered. "Hey, I need you to try and find any others. All right?"

The man shrugged and walked in the direction of the main plane wreckage. "This'll make us even, buddy!" he called.

Clone 71 grinned weakly. "Yeah," he said half-heartedly. "Yeah."

Clone 71 turned back toward the line of wounded clones. Carefully, he examined RG Clone's ruined armor, trying to find a wound. Fortunately, there was none, so he moved on to the young man next to him.

After a quick check, Clone 71 could only find a bandaged wound on the man's thigh, so he confirmed that this was Clone 13.

Clone 71 turned as the only other conscious man returned, carrying a body on his back. Clone 71 swallowed hard.

"Is he dead?" he asked.

The man nodded grimly. "Yup. He's dead, all right." He dumped the body unceremoniously onto the ground and held out his right hand. "I'm Han. I used to be called Clone 56, but I'll go by Han."

Clone 71 shook the outstretched hand. "I'm Clone 71. I *want* to go by Alexander or Steve."

Behind him, RG Clone stirred and sat up. "Whoa, whoa, whoa! What's going on here?"

Clone 71 helped him up. "This is RG Clone. And this," he pointed at Clone 13, "is my injured friend, Clone 13. His leg got shot trying to escape."

Han scowled. "Those damn fools," he said with a growl. "Can't they see what those twins have done?"

RG Clone grimaced in pain. "Yes," he said. "They probably can."

Han and Clone 71 stared at him.

"But they just don't *want* to believe it," finished RG Clone hurriedly, noting the expressions on their faces.

Clone 71 smiled. "Or they don't know because…"

Han cut him off. "Honestly, you two. Get to work! We have men to heal!"

Clone 71 threw a mock salute. "Aye, aye sir."

RG Clone followed his example. "Right away, sir!"

Han laughed. "Shut up! We have a job to do!"

Ten minutes later, Clone 13 and the young purple-haired man had woken up. The young man said he was Brett, the co-pilot of the now wrecked plane. He said that he was an inexperienced pilot and had crashed the plane when trying to land.

Clone 13 was in excellent condition. His thigh wound was healing extremely fast, and there was no sign of infection.

That night, the men slept on the cold, hard floor of the cargo hold. There was no food, so the clones felt extremely weak after not eating for a day. They all slipped away into dreamless sleep, disregarding their fear and terror of the prospects of the journey.

Their plane had gone down. Clone 13 had been injured. Only two of the unfortunate things that had happened to the group of escapees.

But the worst was yet to come!

Chapter 6
Prey and Predators

Clone 71 woke up suddenly; breathing hard and sweat pouring down his neck. He had just had a horribly vivid dream of his comrades dying. One by one, they fell. Blood pouring from wounds in heads, stomachs, and chests…

Clone 71 got up and walked among the sleeping escapees, gently nudging them and beckoning them to follow him outside. They silently got up and followed him.

Once they were outside, the men began to gather their weapons and clip them to their armor. Clone 71 picked up his blaster rifle and held it ready, watching for any movement on the horizon.

The men finished, so Clone 71 beckoned to them again and began to walk away from the wreckage.

In a matter of minutes, the terrain changed into a hot desert with flat terrain and high sandstone cliffs. Clone 71 tightened his grip on his weapon as they passed a skeleton slumped against the wall of a cliff.

They had traveled well into the afternoon when Clone 71 stopped them.

"We'll stop here," said Clone 71 commandingly. "We need rest."

All of the clones collapsed into the sand, some muttering praise to God for giving them rest. Others complained of their sore legs and ankles.

Suddenly, a laser bolt thudded into the ground next to RG Clone and disappeared. RG Clone scrambled up, cursing.

"Snipers!" he yelled. "Try to shoot them!"

Clone 71 rolled aside just as another beam landed where his head had been a millisecond before.

"Aha!" he said loudly, startling the others in the group. "There you are!"

He pulled his blaster rifle off his belt and aimed toward the small glint of metal that he saw. He fired off twelve shots, and then waited.

A scream rented the air, then silence.

"Got one," said Clone 71, grinning. "He won't be bothering us again." He tripped and fell on a rock.

Brett looked up toward the cliff again. "Hey, guys, I think that there's one left," he voiced.

"Yeah," said Han, nodding his head furiously.

A laser beam hit the ground next to Brett's foot.

"RUN!" Clone 71 yelled as Brett tripped and fell in the dust.

RG Clone pulled Brett up and sprinted as laser beams hit the ground next to them.

Han slowed down to let RG Clone and Brett catch up. As RG Clone and Brett raced past, a perfectly aimed beam connected with the back of Han's head. Without a sound, Han fell to the ground, dead.

They had run for quite a while when they finally stopped and made camp. Clone 71 counted the men.

"Guys, there are only four of us," observed Clone 71. "Where's Han?"

The other three clones shook their heads. "No idea," said RG Clone innocently.

"I think I know."

All eyes fell onto Brett. "He must have been shot when he waited for us to catch up. After we passed him, the snipers probably shot him."

Clone 71 bowed his head.

That night, Clone 71 watched the camp. Thunder and lightning streaked across the sky. Somehow, rain was nonexistent.

"NO!"

Chapter 7
A Growing Suspicion

When the clones woke up and took off their armor, Clone 71 couldn't help but notice that they were all looking horrible. They hadn't had water for almost three days now. Clone 71 knew that all of them were hanging on a thread. Living two days without water was a sure feat, but *three*? No way.

Red circles were under the eyes of all of them. The one who looked best was Brett. He wasn't even thirsty or hungry. Not even tired.

A small suspicion nudged into Clone 71's mind, but he dismissed it quickly. No way. He would never…

Clone 71 cleared his throat, making all of the clones turn toward him.

"All right, guys. We are going to die without food or water, so we need to move as fast as we can. Leave your armor here, but take your weapons and belt. Now come on!" he commanded. "Let's move!"

After walking for an hour or so, RG Clone suddenly ran ahead of them, yelling and laughing insanely. Clone 71 gestured to the men. "Follow him," he said, grinning. "I think he's found something."

After a while, RG Clone slowed and stopped, shocked.

RG Clone was standing next to an oasis. Three palm trees were in the middle of a pool of freshwater. A solitary sheep was grazing on the little grass that surrounded the lake.

All of the clones stuck their heads into the cool water, slurping up buckets of it.

After having his drink, RG Clone used his blaster rifle to shoot coconuts off of the palm trees, knocking them across the water into Clone 13's arms.

Clone 71 started a fire, killed the sheep, and roasted it over the fire.

Brett sat around and let the other clones work, drink, and eat.

By night, the young men were full of delicious meat, coconuts, and water. They all slept soundly that night.

All except one.

Chapter 8
Betrayal!

Brett woke up very early. He ate a short meal of fresh cooked biscuits and red meat. He smiled. If any of the escapees would survive, it would be him. He started a small fire, and then walked away from the sleeping clones toward the north.

After a while, Brett reached a large steel building with no visible doorway. Brett felt the wall with his hands. The steel was freezing except for one hotspot on the bottom edge of the wall. Brett knocked four times on the hotspot and waited expectantly.

Suddenly, a hole appeared in the wall. Brett jumped into it and allowed himself to be pulled up by an invisible arm. Suddenly, he was dragged onto a polished marble floor.

"Ah," said an oily voice. "Brett. Any news?"
Brett got up slowly, rubbing his sore limbs.
"Yes, Commander. They are resting at the oasis. They will probably rest until eight."

The oily-voiced man came into his view. "Go to them," said the man. "We will follow and kill them all."

Brett nodded. "Yes sir."

An hour later, Brett returned to the camp. He hid behind a palm tree and watched as Clone 71 stirred and got up, back facing Brett.

Brett didn't miss a step as he left his hiding place and readied his blaster rifle. Unfortunately for him, Brett didn't notice RG Clone watching with half-closed lids.

Brett ran toward Clone 71 and raised his blaster rifle. Just as he was going to fire his weapon, RG Clone fired his.

Brett cried out as the blaster shot hit him in the head. He fell to the ground, limp.

Clone 71 whipped around, raising his blaster rifle. "What happened?" he asked loudly.

RG Clone gave a humorless chuckle. "Brett. He ran at you from behind, but I nailed him."

Clone 71 pointed the muzzle of his blaster rifle at RG Clone. "Put the gun down now!" commanded Clone 71. "Or I'll nail…"

Brett jumped up and punched the clone in the face. Clone 71 reeled back against a palm tree, dropping his rifle. As he wiped blood away from his face, another punch sent him sailing into the lake.

RG Clone aimed his blaster rifle at Brett, but he was too quick. Darting under the crosshairs, he attempted to tackle RG Clone. But the royal guard's grueling training was too much to conquer. Gripping the back of Brett's shirt, RG Clone spun several times, making his weight swing around quickly. When he released his burden, Brett rocketed across the lake like a cannon, slammed into a rock solid palm tree, and bounced back another few feet to land in the lake, limp.

Dusting off his clothes, RG Clone ran to the edge of the lake and helped a coughing and choking Clone 71 out of the water.

"What the…" sputtered Clone 71.

"No," RG Clone cut in. "Lie down."

But Clone 71 pushed him away. "If Brett was a traitor, he wouldn't plan to kill us one by one. He would bring pals." He stood up. "Wake Clone 13; we need to move. Fast."

Five minutes later, the three men were on the move again. They walked away from the oasis into a sandstorm.

Unknown to the men, ten clones marched only 30 feet behind, but in the storm, couldn't be heard.

They marched long into the night. As the storm subsided, their ten followers fell farther behind, until they couldn't be seen by the naked eye.

Finally, at midnight, Clone 71 called a rest. The exhausted clones wearily collapsed onto the ground, gasping for breath. Slowly, they all fell asleep, one by one.

However, Clone 71 was still awake. His eyes were riveted on something visible in the distance.

A skyscraper.

Chapter 9
Trouble

At dawn, RG Clone and Clone 13 were rudely awakened by gentle kicks from Clone 71. As they stood up, rubbing their eyes and swearing, they saw the towering building in the distance. They both stopped in the middle of their movements.

"Wow," said RG Clone.

"Good Lord," breathed Clone 13. "How was that built?"

Clone 71 shook his head, exasperated. "Guys, let's move. We have a brigade chasing us."

RG Clone laughed. "Brigade? What brigade?"

As they talked, seventy-five clones were creeping along, unnoticed, completely surrounding them.

Clone 13 began to walk toward the skyscraper, pulling out his pistol and holding it dramatically. "And now, for James Bond's final act. Bond, center stage!"

Clone 71 started rolling on the ground with laughter. RG Clone grabbed him and pulled him back onto his feet, chuckling.

Suddenly, the brigade of clones stood up and pointed their blaster rifles at them.

Clone 71 ripped his blaster rifle off of his belt and chose a target. RG Clone raised his pistol, but he dropped it as a heavy punch floored him. Clone 13 was seized and disarmed.

All eyes were on Clone 71. He hadn't moved yet.

A young clone wearing black armor inched toward Clone 71 from behind. Clone 71 heard the man, but kept his position. Just as the man drew his arm back for a punch, Clone 71 grabbed his throat and pulled him in.

"If you don't let my friends go," he yelled, gesturing toward the man in black armor, "he dies."

"Whatever," a voice said. "Kill his friends. Show no mercy."

Clone 71 lowered his blaster rifle and pulled out a knife, putting it to the man's throat. "I'll rip him apart!" he yelled. "He'll be little pieces if you don't let my friends go!"

"Ah," said the voice again. "I presume that I must compromise with you."

A young man with jet black hair strode from the back of the group. "Here is my deal. You and your friends must leave. You will give me everything you have. Deal?"
Clone 71 took a step forward. "Deal."
The man smiled. "Release him."
Clone 71 pressed the knife against the man's throat. "No. Not until my friends are released." The man smiled more. "No deal then."
Clone 71 hardly had time to protest before a fist slammed into his nose and veils of black fell across his eyes. He fell to the ground, limp.

Chapter 10
Rescued!

Several hours later, Clone 71 finally lifted from his unconsciousness. Strangely, he thought he was standing. Turning his head, Clone 71 saw that he had been tied to a large oak tree. Craning his neck even farther, he could see RG Clone tied on the opposite side of the tree.

Something pricked him on the arm. Clone 71 saw RG Clone straining to give him a knife. Clone 71 gripped the blade of the knife and pulled it away from RG Clone. He started sawing at his bonds.

A campfire burnt in the middle of a depression in the earth. Next to it were several guards and a bound Clone 13.

A guard got up from next to the fire, drew a pistol, and ambled over to the tree where the clones were tied. He turned his back to them, and then stopped.

Clone 71 cut his body free and turned to remove RG Clone's bonds.

Suddenly, the knife slipped and cut RG Clone's finger. He cried out.

The guard turned, but Clone 71 was already upon him. He landed a perfect punch on the man's throat, making him gasp for breath and drop his pistol. Clone 71 scooped up a sonic grenade lying next to the gasping guard and threw it at the campfire.

The grenade hit the middle of the campfire and detonated, throwing ash and coal everywhere. All the guards caught fire, but Clone 13 miraculously stayed extinguished, rolling away from the explosion.

RG Clone wriggled free from his bonds and took the knife to untie Clone 13.

All of the guards ran away, some with their heads engulfed in flames. Clone 71 chuckled and turned to find Clone 13 and RG Clone untied and ready to march.

Clone 71 nodded in the direction of the more distant skyscraper. "Come on then, men. We are doing well. We are almost out of clone controlled territory."

RG Clone grimaced. "We best move fast, or they'll find us."

The clones walked off toward the distant building, grimacing.

Several hours later, night had long since fallen, and the skyscraper could still be seen, despite the fact that no lights illuminated it.

"We're close now," muttered Clone 13. "Very close."

Clone 71 suddenly jumped up and down, pointing. "There's the base! It's right there!"

One hundred fifty yards away, the steel base of the skyscraper glinted. Clone 71 gazed at it in awe, taking a step forward.

Suddenly, red laser bolts whizzed out from behind them.

"Run for your lives!" yelled Clone 71, stepping on the gas and sprinting ahead of his two bewildered companions, who began to run as well.

Clone 71 looked back and ran harder.

A veritable army of clones, about one thousand of them, were chasing them down with top notch blaster rifles and rocket launchers. Guided rocket launchers.

Now only fifty yards from the building, Clone 71 pushed himself harder as green sniper bolts whizzed by his ear. Clone 13 and RG Clone had now caught up to him, running as one toward the ever nearing building.

Ten, five, three yards now. Clone 71 slammed through a window and catapulted into a wall. Dazed, he got up and pressed a button on the wall.

A turbolift next to the button opened, and Clone 71 collapsed into it. Clone 13 and RG Clone dove through the doors and pressed the close button. But a single sniper bolt slipped through and hit Clone 71's arm.

Clone 71 screamed at the top of his lungs. He entered a spasm of kicking and writhing, but slowed down as he entered unconsciousness. Clone 13 tended to him as RG Clone waited for the elevator to reach its destination.

Chapter 11
Genies in Blue Bottles

Clone 71 was swimming in a black pool of emptiness. He could hear nothing but a distant voice that wavered in his head. "71," he heard. "Leave this place, 71."

He felt himself rising from the pool and vanishing in a flash of light…

"Wake up, brother; it's on in the afternoon. You haven't eaten in two days."

Clone 71's eyes snapped open. RG Clone was watching him, smiling.

"Eat some of this," he said, gesturing to a plate of eggs piled with pepper. "This food is good."

Clone 71 tried to sit up, his arm searing, but RG Clone pushed him down.

"Wait," he said. "Let me recline your seat."

RG Clone pressed a button on the wall and Clone 71's seat pushed him into a sitting position.

"Eat, fool. You'll die if you don't." RG Clone held out the plate. Clone 71 picked it up with his non-injured arm, set it down, and took the fork that was presented to him. He then began to eat.

"Where are we anyway?" asked Clone 71 curiously. "A room in the skyscraper?"

"No," said RG Clone, annoyed.

"Where then?"

"All right, get this," exclaimed RG Clone. "There is a city on top of the skyscraper!"

"So?" snorted Clone 71. He then smiled. "Just joking, that's cool!"

"We are in the D Block," said RG Clone informatively. "That's where all of the public services are."

Clone 71 licked the last of the eggs off the plate and swallowed. "This is good stuff."

"Don't thank me. Thank the head hospital cook." RG Clone said professionally.

"You're cooking knowledge is too limited to cook eggs," scoffed Clone 71 jokingly. "Why would I ever think of thanking you?"

They both laughed. Everyone in the old cloning complex skipped breakfast if RG Clone was cooking it.

RG Clone cleared his throat loudly. "The smiths polished and cleaned our weapons. Here they are." He pulled a gleaming rifle out of his belt. "As a gift, they also gave you this." RG Clone handed him a blue bottle. "They say it is good in times of need. Probably some spicy substance that perks you up, but nothing more."

He raised a hand and waved to Clone 71. "See you later!" said RG Clone as he left the room.

Now that his strength was replenished, Clone 71 slid off of the bed and stood up shakily as he explored his room. He opened a drawer and found some clothes neatly folded inside. He took out a blue polo shirt and a pair of pants with a belt and showered in the bathroom next door. He shaved and dressed, then left his room to explore this strange place.

When he left his room, the clone found himself in a long corridor that opened up into a large room filled with people. The clone was bewildered at all of the guards, and even more surprised when several of them moved and guarded the black door straight across the room from him. "Strange," Clone 71 muttered softly. "Very strange."

Opening a door to his left, Clone 71 found himself under the mild stare of the sun. Smiling, he went back through the door.

Strangely enough, the guards were gone from the black door. Clone 71 ducked low and crept toward it. Turning the handle slowly, he sprang the door open and slipped in, without any notice.

He found himself in a tall, rectangular room filled with glass bottles filled with the same blue substance in his bottle. He picked up a bottle of it and popped the cap. Sniffing the liquid, he found no disturbing scent. He lifted it to his lips and drank a deep draught.

A fiery feeling burst through his body, filling every part of him, expanding, ever expanding…

It was over almost before it had begun. Clone 71 noticed no changes to his body. Shrugging, he walked away, leaving the empty bottle on the shelf.

Chapter 12
Skyscraper City

Clone 71 woke up the next day feeling extra chipper. He didn't know what was changing him, but he was sure that it was the blue bottle.

Besides, he had drunk the whole thing. He'd be dead if he drank poison. But feeling extra good? No way.

He moved in with RG Clone and Clone 13, and they now lived in a small house connected to the hospital. Clone 71 hadn't seen the city yet, so he left the house to walk around in the streets.

He opened the door and stepped outside into the cool breeze. Rubbing his hands together, the young clone began to walk down the silent street.

The place was a technological marvel, from the titanium rapid-fire blaster rifles to the little robotic booths that would open up in the street, fill with fruits and vegetables, and zoom around to sell them. The guards wore top-notch armor that could stop a blaster bolt dead in its tracks.

The streets began to fill with people, and soon, it was full of them. Clone 71 struggled against the flow of the crowd toward a small, rickety shop that traffic had not touched yet.

He reached the building and opened the door. An old man carrying a cane beckoned him inside.
"Your two other friends are here," he cackled, grinning crookedly and motioning toward a table. At the table sat Clone 13 and RG Clone. Both were sulking.

Clone 71 sat down at the silent table and smiled. "What now?" he said cheerfully.

Clone 13 looked at him glumly. "We need to go back and rescue them."

Clone 71 shrugged. "Who?"

RG Clone sat up. "Our clone pals. Those Schwartz brothers are going to brainwash those clones. It has something to do with this place."

Clone 13 shook his head. "No way. We should go and save those clones."

RG Clone turned his head, disgusted. "Hero," he muttered.

Clone 71 slapped him. "Come on," he exclaimed. "We get allies and go blow up the place. And save the clones that are in there." He added, pointing at Clone 13.

"The army here could help us!" said Clone 13 excitedly, snapping his fingers. "We could go in, blow up the place, and get out."

Clone 71 already was nodding. "Yeah," he said, turning to RG Clone. "That is a good idea."

RG Clone shook his head. "How though? We hardly know these people. They won't give us permission for pretty much anything, much less to use their army!"

Clone 71 smiled. "We talk to the Big Cheese. Simple."

Clone 13 stood up with a grunt. "Where is this cheese then?"

RG Clone slid out of his chair and stood. "We'll find him."

Far away from them, in the clone facility, the Schwartz brothers conversed softly as they walked through the empty corridors.

"Some of the clones escaped," James Schwartz hissed softly. "They are in Skyscraper City. Our armies have tried for days to get up there, but the turbolifts won't work."

Michael Schwartz sighed and turned away from his brother. "Will you ever understand that they aren't important? We have around a million clones being made, what are your worries?"

James stopped walking for a moment. "Clone 71, RG Clone, and Clone 13 are some of my first clones. They were made to be very resourceful. I fear we will be taken down by their abilities."

Michael shrugged and walked ahead of him. "We'll see," he muttered. "We'll see."

Chapter 13
No Choice

Clone 13 got up early and searched for his shoes. He found them on the ground near his bed and put them on. He wanted to find the head of this place.

He walked into the hospital. The rooms were all empty, no one inside. He shrugged and entered the main room. He walked to a turbolift and pressed the down button.

"Ding!" The door opened, and Clone 13 stepped inside. Pressing floor fifty, he smiled as the turbolift began going down.

At the bottom of the skyscraper, the clone engineers fiddled with wires on the turbolift.

"They started it," they yelled joyfully. "We'll change the route to this floor!"

They cut one of the wires and connected it to a computer. They typed in the command to change the route.

Clone 13 finally noticed that it had been a while since the turbolift had started going down. He looked at the numbers on the wall.

Ten, nine, eight, seven…"

"What?" he exclaimed. "I'm going to the…"

Three, two…

He pulled a small metal cylinder from his belt, which lengthened to a blaster rifle.

One…

"Ding!"

"Prepare to die," he muttered as the doors opened.

Clone 71 woke up shivering with fear and breathing hard. Sweat made his skin glisten and glow eerily in the dim light. He ripped off his covers and lay there, cooling off, as his heart slowed. He remained like this for several minutes. Slowly, he sat up and pulled a t-shirt on and shrugged on some jet blue armor hanging neatly on his bedpost. "Funny people, these guys," he thought. "They give you free armor."

Smiling to himself, he tapped RG Clone and Clone 13 awake.

Or did he?

He felt only sheets in Clone 13's bed. He tapped RG Clone again, harder this time.

"All right," RG Clone grunted softly. "I'm getting up." He slowly stood. "What?"

Clone 71 only pointed at Clone 13's empty bed. RG Clone gaped.

Pulling on his armor and strapping his weapons to his belt, RG Clone quickly suited up. He tossed Clone 71 his weapons and sped out the door. After fastening on his weapons, Clone 71 did the same.

They looked left and right for Clone 13. No sign. They ran back into their room and went into the hospital. Running down the corridor, they entered the main room. Looking at the turbolift, they looked at each other and communicated the same thing.

Clone 13 was dead.

They didn't dare take the lift, because they would probably end up facing one hundred clones in battle. Not a good idea.

"What's that?" asked RG Clone.

A small noise was getting closer and closer to them. "It's just the lift," said Clone 71. "It's probably clones. Ready your weapon."

RG Clone took a long, slender cylinder from his belt, which lengthened and turned into a double-bladed electro-sword. Clone 71 readied his blaster rifle.

The lift stopped and the doors opened. Several clones jumped out and immediately assaulted them. RG Clone was disarmed and thrown across the room to hit the wall, unconscious. Clone 71 had killed three and was in the process of knocking out a young clone with his rifle when a hand gripped the scruff of his neck and threw him across the room to join RG Clone. When he hit the wall, he also slammed into a red button and pushed it in, unnoticed.

Nothing happened, though, so Clone 71 got up again, only to be punched in the face and fall face-down. As his mind began to dim, he took out his blue bottle and took a brief sip.

The burst of energy came, and Clone 71 jumped up and kicked a clone in the face, sending him reeling.

Unnoticed, a clone sharpshooter readied his sniper rifle and fired directly at Clone 71's chest.

Clone 71 turned just as the laser beam slammed into his head. Time seemed to freeze as he waited for the blood to cascade down. But strangely, there was no blood, and the laser bounced off of his undamaged head and hit the sniper in the chest, killing him.

Clone 71 stood there, shocked, as more lasers flew off his body and bounced into enemy heads and chests. After only a few seconds, the battle was over, as all of the clones had been killed by their own shots.

He ran over to RG Clone and woke him with a gentle slap. "Hey, RG Clone, wake up."

RG Clone's eyes opened and he stood up shakily. "What the…?"

But his question remained unanswered as security came around the corner and escorted them away from the scene.

Chapter 13
The Quest

Clone 71 and RG Clone were led through some double doors into a study.

One of the guards saluted a chair. "Sir, we brought the men who hit the alarm."

The chair swiveled and a tall, thin man stood up and saluted the guard. "As to you, my good friend," he said in a kind, old voice. "Sit down, friends. Guards, leave us." He gestured to two seats in front of his desk and shooed away the guards.

The clones both sat down.

"So," the man said inquisitively. "What brings you here?"

Clone 71's eyes were downcast as he said, "Our clone friend, Clone 13."

The man smote his forehead. "How I forget things! What are your names?"

Clone 71 gestured to RG Clone. "This is RG Clone. I am Clone 71."

"Ah," the man said. "Our new visitors. How did you come here anyway?"

"We escaped the underground cloning facility owned by the Schwartz brothers. They are planning to brainwash their clones and make them into an army," said Clone 71.

The man scowled. "They plot to take over this whole government! I control half of the sky, and I have this and that to worry about, and then Michael Schwartz comes along and attacks my country! He's a darn devil, that's for sure!"

Clone 71 nodded. "He is precisely that. However, I want to get my friend back!"

"He kidnapped your friend?" asked the man. "How?"

"We're not sure, sir," replied RG Clone. "But we know they have him and will move back to their base. If we don't rescue him and all of the other clones, we'll all die."

The man shrugged. "I see your point. You want my army, take it. Take it all. Just get the clones off my darn doorstep!"

"Yes, sir," said RG Clone sharply. He and Clone 71 both stood up and left the room silently.

After they left, Clone 71 turned to RG Clone. "All we need to do is figure out how to blow that whole place up and then we're going on a little trip back to the clone facility!"

Chapter 14
Commanders

Clone 71 and RG Clone woke up early and dressed. They pulled on all of their armor and hooked every weapon they owned to their belts.

After suiting up, the two clones walked outside to give their army orders.

The whole army was massed outside. They filled the street, every nook and cranny.

It was huge, but not huge enough. Despite its size, Clone 71 knew it wouldn't be enough. However, he still strode toward the front rank with confidence.

"All right," he yelled. "Follow us and take the turbolifts down. I'll meet you there. Divide into squadrons and follow us. One squad per elevator. Let's move, now!"

The soldiers followed the two clones, toward the main building and its turbolifts.

Four clones were sitting down, facing the main elevator. They all were eating their lunches of turkey and chicken sandwiches.

One of the clones sighed and dropped his sandwich. "Honestly, guys, we shouldn't be doing this. This is boring. And besides, Clone 25 told us that the Schwartz twins were planning something, and he ended up dead."

Another clone spat on the ground. "Yeah, I was Clone 71's roommate, and he left the place and never came back."

"Good point, Clone 11. Let's join their group if they come," said a stocky older man.

"Ding!" The turbolift doors opened and several soldiers came out, pointing their blaster rifles at the clones. Clone 71 and

RG Clone came out as well, pointing their rifles at the clones, who put their hands up high and dropped their weapons.

"Hey!" said Clone 11, his hands outstretched, shielding his face from the muzzle of Clone 71's rifle.

Clone 71 looked down the barrel, then dropped his weapon and hugged the man. "Hey buddy," he exclaimed happily. "How are you? Still sleepy?"

The man patted his back and smiled, pulling away. "Yeah, a little,"

RG Clone smiled and clapped the rest of the clones on the back.

"We have rooms in the skyscraper, if you want," said Clone 71.

All of them walked toward the turbolift except one. Clone 11 picked up his blaster rifle and walked out the door of the skyscraper at a brisk pace.

Clone 71 grinned. "Come on men. Time to go."

They all set off after the figure of Clone 11, moving hastily to catch up with him.

Several hours later, the sun set, casting a stunningly beautiful pink and crimson color across the sky. The clones ordered them to set up camp in a small wood next to a cliff. The soldiers collapsed onto the ground, grateful for the stop. Rations were broken out, and the soldiers ate with relish, watching the amazing sunset conclude.

Clone 71 stood on a small hill, watching the young men. A breeze ruffled his hair lightly as he smiled contentedly. This was a good day. They had covered a lot of ground today, and the weather was cool. As light faded from the sky and disappeared, Clone 71 leaned against a tree and fell asleep to the sound of birds chirping softly.

Chapter 15
Finding a Way

Clone 71 woke up slowly, stretching and yawning. It was rather late, and the sun had already risen. Rubbing his sore back, he stood up and swept his eyes over the busy, but quiet camp. He nodded his head approvingly as a soldier bearing a tray of food walked over to him and silently served him a bowl of oatmeal and bread. He took the meal gratefully and ate, relishing the taste. After his breakfast, he found Clone 11 and RG Clone packing up their supplies and weapons for the march. He patted them both on the back and smiled.

"Good job, guys," said Clone 71. "When you're done, we need to get out of here."

Clone 11 straightened up. "I'm done."

RG Clone strapped on his armor. "Me too."

"Let's go, then," said Clone 71. "Get your squads and get them on the move.

Ten minutes later, they were on their way. The army was several thousand strong, but the three clones knew that their enemy outnumbered them almost twenty to one.

Clone 71 took a sip of water. "So," he said seriously. "How are we going to blow up the clone facility?"

Clone 11 shook his head. "Not possible. The only way would be to blow the nuclear reactors, but that would be easily contained by closing off the passages with the security system blast doors."

"How do you know all this stuff?" asked Clone 71 in awe.

"I'm an engineer," replied Clone 11, puffing up his chest. "I work in the security section. I know the whole place."

RG Clone laughed sarcastically. "Right. Then HOW do we blow up the facility?"

Clone 11 tapped his chin knowledgeably, and then suddenly brightened. "I know! The clones are building a new wing in the facility. They just put in a building that controls the automatic defense systems. If we blow that up, the whole place would be undefended."

"Who cares?" asked a nearby soldier. "All you need to do is hack the system and change the code to disable all of the security and the nuclear blast doors."

Clone 71 turned toward him. "The blast doors are controlled by a self-generated defense system. If you mess with the code on the main security system, the blast doors automatically close and cut the code, activating the shields. If that happens, we'll never get in there."

RG Clone smiled. "It's obvious."

The clones turned toward him. "What?"

"If you plant explosives in the water pipes, the explosives will travel to the sewer. Where is the sewer? Under the facility. If you blow up all of that flammable material, that's a big explosion," said RG Clone, shaking his head. "They filter the water with laser, not like the old filters that we used to use. They kill unhealthy microbes in the water, not a bomb."

Clone 71 laughed loudly and jumped up and down. "We got it!"

Clone 11 started dancing around and laughing.

RG Clone watched his dancing companions and shook his head again, smiling. "Come on, guys," he called. "You'll fall behind!"

The two clones quickly returned to formation and kept marching, smiling as they went.

Chapter 16
Confrontation

The next day, Clone 71 woke up and ate early. He had a meager meal of one egg and a sip of water because of the need to conserve food.

He poked his two companions awake and then began his lookout shift at their hot, dry, but sheltered campsite. It was cool at this time, but it would become hotter when the sun came up.

Clone 11 came up next to him. "What are you going to do when this is over?" he asked Clone 71 softly.

Clone 71 shrugged. "I don't know."

Clone 11 smiled sadly. "If we will be here anymore," he said.

Clone 71 turned and looked him in the eye. "You are not going to die. Neither are RG Clone and Clone 13…" His voice trailed off as Clone 11 walked away from him.

Clone 71 sighed and turned forward again, ignoring him. "It was my idea to rescue the clones and Clone 13," he said to himself. "I guess this is entirely my fault."

He laid his blaster rifle on the ground and sat down. He ran a hand through his hair, stressed. "Why am I the one to have all of this trouble? I have to rescue Clone 13 and the clones. I have to!" He looked up to see something move ten feet in front of him. He straightened quickly, frightened, and grabbed his blaster rifle. He slowly advanced toward the spot.

Nothing. He took a hand from his rifle and wiped his sweaty brow. It must have been an animal.

Suddenly, a figure sprang from the ground in front of him and tackled him around the waist, making Clone 71 drop his weapon. The rifle skittered several feet from them and stopped.

Clone 71 struggled to push his attacker off of him, but he couldn't. He felt himself being pulled away from the camp, his weapon getting farther and farther away.

Then, he got an idea. Clone 71 twisted and smacked the figure in the right place.

His attacker yelled in pain and loosened his grip. Seizing his opportunity, Clone 71 wriggled free from the man's grasp and got up. He sprinted toward his rifle, desperate for a defense. Clone 11 was too far away to notice that something was wrong, so he couldn't call for aid.

Now a few feet away, his weapon glinted. He gathered his strength and dove towards it.

He grabbed the handle and pulled it up. He had almost opened fire on his enemy when a force grenade hit the ground next to him and detonated, blasting him several yards into the air. His rifle again clattered down several feet away.

Clone 71 turned painfully and faced his attacker, who was standing right above him. His fancy helmet and armor made him look intimidating.

Clone 71 raised his hands in surrender. "I give up. What do you want?"

The gloved hands pulled out a laser pistol and pointed it into his face. "I want your life!" he said. His finger tightened on the trigger just as Clone 71 unhooked a force grenade from his own belt and threw it at the man.

The grenade detonated when it touched the shiny armor. The man was thrown fifty feet back and slumped onto the ground, unconscious because of the beating he had just taken.

Clone 71 stood up painfully and limped to his blaster rifle and picked it up slowly. He gave out from the effort and fell to the ground, recuperating from his use of energy.

Clone 11 saw the blue flash of Clone 71's force grenade, and he came running. He watched as his friend attempted to pick up his weapon and slumped to the ground. He ran over to him, picked him up cautiously, and took him to the encampment to wait for the sun to come out.

Chapter 17
Trouble in the Desert

Clone 71 awoke slowly from his stupor. He tried to sit up, but a hand pushed him down.

"Stay still, buddy," said RG Clone.

"Heck with that," argued Clone 71, breaking his grasp and standing. Slightly dizzy, he observed the sky. It was clear and bright, with no clouds floating around.

Retrieving his blaster rifle from the ground next to him and clipping it to his belt, Clone 71 clapped RG Clone on the back and pushed him toward the rest of the tents.

"RG Clone, we need to move! Get the troops together!" commanded Clone 71.

RG Clone nodded contritely and walked off.

Clone 71 satisfied himself with a grin and turned to see Clone 11.

"Clone 71," asked Clone 11. "What's going on?"

He nodded. "About that, RG Clone is organizing the soldiers now; I expect them to be assembled any moment now."

Clone 11 smiled. "Great, that solves it. I'll go help." He scurried off toward the increasing mass of troops over near the now folding tents.

Clone 71's eyes swept the terrain. He couldn't see anything but a blob of white in the distance. What was that anyway?

"Sir," called a voice behind him. "The soldiers are ready."

Clone 71 turned toward a shaking private who couldn't have been more than fifteen years old. "All right. Thanks."

The private saluted, shaking considerably less now, and led him to his fully assembled army.

They were already split into squads for him, so Clone 71 had no work to do but to send them on the march. He waved a hand into the air and signaled his troops to move. Then, the march began.

Clone 71 could still see that blob of white on the horizon; it was getting to be much bigger. Was that… an attack force?

Clone 71 conversed quickly with Clone 11 and RG Clone. They all agreed. But it was too late.

The enemy was now clearly visible. It was a large platoon of clones, fitted with blaster rifles. But in the middle of the group, there was a huge vehicle that stopped them in their tracks.

A mighty machine the size of the largest elephant was tramping towards them on its six heavy legs. Snipers were kneeling on top of it, and the vehicle itself carried several cannons whose barrels Clone 71 could fit into. Worst of all, it carried a huge guided missile and a force grenade cannon.

The soldiers drew their weapons bravely, but they still shook in fear. The vehicle alone would devastate half of their forces at least.

A tall man next to Clone 71 drew a rocket launcher from his belt. "Watch this," he said, and fired.

The rocket shot flew high into the sky, disappearing from view.

"Wait," said the man.

The rocket came down so fast onto the vehicle that no one saw it. It plummeted through it, killing all but one sniper and wounding all of the pilots. Despite the destruction, the vehicle still stood.

Renewed, the soldiers attacked the surprised clones vigorously, firing their rifles as if in a frenzy. The clones quickly regained their senses and fought back, but the soldiers had already overpowered them.

Then, one hundred clones sprang from hiding behind the vehicle. They were all snipers, equipped with high-power DS-99 beam sniper rifles. If they fired from this range, the laser beam would kill two men at once.

The soldiers hesitated for a moment, and then retreated. Clones fired after them, picking off the stragglers in the disorganized group.

Clone 71 was knocked to the ground in the stampede of soldiers. He struggled up, then found himself alone facing hundreds of clones. They all aimed their weapons at him.

Clone 71 attempted to grin and dropped his blaster rifle. "Hi guys," he said lamely. "What's up?"

One of the clones walked up to him and tapped the barrel of his sniper rifle against Clone 71's chest. "Come on," he said. "You're a prisoner."

Clone 71 reached for the blue bottle hanging from his belt. "I'm thirsty," he whimpered.

"Fine, drink up," said the clone. "We can't wait all day."

Out of the corner of his eye, Clone 71 saw the soldiers moving around the clone's encampment warily. RG Clone and Clone 11 were leading them cautiously.

Clone 71 took a long draught from the bottle, and the familiar fiery feeling attacked his body. He picked up his blaster rifle and ran towards his men.

All of the snipers fired at Clone 71, and they all hit their target. Oddly enough, the beams bounced right back off of him and killed their owner.

The clones were in a state of chaos. Their reinforcements were depleted, and no one was anxious to die first. They all scrambled toward the still operational vehicle, trying to use their last opportunity of survival.

After a long run, Clone 71 caught up with his group. "Whatever you can do to hurry, do it," he panted. "Th…"

"BOOM!" A roar from the vehicle sent a force bolt into the ground next to Clone 71.

He flew high into the air, almost thirty feet above the ground, and then hit the ground hard. Pain exploded in his chest. He couldn't move anything. He couldn't keep his eyes from closing…

Chapter 18
The Remnant

Clone 71 revived slowly and painfully. His chest hurt every time he breathed. His left hand was immobile and throbbed as well. He still couldn't move.

It was midnight. The cool air felt good after such a long time in the desert heat. Clone 71 watched the sky full of stars. He tried to pick out the constellations. The sky was so beautiful, as was life.

He heard a noise nearby, but couldn't tell what it was because his head was refusing to move. He struggled for another breath, and rattled, "Help me."

A crunch of rocks, and then RG Clone was at his side. "Clone 71," he exclaimed. "You look awful! What happened?"

Clone 71 was speechless except for a noisy sucking sound.

"Ribs, eh?" RG Clone grimaced. "Okay, I'll carry you."

Clone 71 remained immobile as RG Clone scooped him up carefully and walked toward a fire.

"There you go," he said. "That'll do." RG Clone lay him down gently next to the fire and drew a knife, a pair of scissors, and some bottles. "Drink up," he said, tipping a teaspoon of liquid into Clone 71's mouth.

He swallowed. "There's no more pain," observed Clone 71.

RG Clone held up the knife and the scissors. "I have to work on you. Stay down."

Clone 71 obliged and allowed him to check his wounds. RG Clone shook his head.

"What have you done? You have broken two ribs and fractured your left wrist. This will take a while," observed RG Clone grimly. "Guys!"

Two men wearing tattered armor stepped into Clone 71's view. "Okay," they said in unison. "We'll be happy to help."

They went to work on him, first picking through the tissue and setting the rib. Luckily, a medical kit was available, so they were able to set his rib with a special tool that melds bones together fast. Then, they entered his wrist. RG Clone picked through the bone and fixed the fracture.

Finally, they finished and closed the skin seamlessly with another tool. The men allowed Clone 71 to stand.

"I feel fine," said Clone 71 happily.

The men nodded, unfazed, while RG Clone clapped him on the back.

"Great, buddy," said RG Clone. "You're back in the game!"

Clone 71's happiness faded. "Is everyone okay?"

RG Clone turned him around toward a group of men behind the campfire.

"You're kidding me, right?" asked Clone 71, uneasy.

RG Clone shook his head. "This is it."

Clone 71 surveyed the small group of men. "There are only eight there. That means…" He swiveled toward RG Clone again, shocked. "Ten guys?"

RG Clone nodded sadly. "Yes."

Clone 71 sat down next to the fire, unwilling to accept the fact that he had almost no chance to get Clone 13 back and destroy the Schwartz brothers.

Clone 11 stepped from the solemn group. "At least you have us," he said.

Clone 71 sighed and lay down. He was too tired to think about it. Now, he would sleep.

He rested his head on the ground and fell asleep, comforted by the fire's warm presence.

Chapter 19
The Facility

"Buddy," said a voice. "Buddy, wake up."

Clone 71 sat up and rubbed the sleep from his eyes to find himself looking at Clone 11 and a dim sky. "What?" he called out dimly.

"Get up!" yelled Clone 11 strictly. "We're burning daylight, now move!"

Clone 71 stood up and snatched his blaster rifle from the ground. "Okay," he said obligingly. "Let's go rouse the others."

The two friends ran off toward the sleeping soldiers and began to nudge them awake.

After everyone was awake, the group set off. There was no breakfast because of the frugal supplies.

The day passed rather quickly, and the sky brightened. After several hours, Clone 71 finally saw the facility.

Only the hanger door showed. It was jet black and easy to spot. It was also secured onto a slight incline.

The group quieted as the rest of the men set their eyes onto the door. They jogged quietly, weapons clinking musically.

Eventually, they reached the door. Everyone tumbled to the ground, tired and hungry. Clone 71 served out their meal and they all began to tear at the food hungrily, despite the frugal amount.

RG Clone burped loudly and lay down next to the hanger doors. "Excuse me," he announced. "So refreshing."

Clone 71 was already done with his food. He began to search for a way in that would be unhindered, since the door was impenetrable by any weapon except an extremely powerful bomb, which they didn't have.

He tripped over something and fell onto the ground hard. He spat out a tooth and got up, swearing. He turned toward the spot and saw something.

A small switch was there. Looking around, he summoned Clone 11.

"What?" Clone 11 asked. "You want me to tell you what this does?"

"Yeah," said Clone 71.

Clone 11 scratched his head. "I'm pretty sure it opens the doors. Try it."

Clone 71 flipped the switch and the ground below them gave way. They both fell noiselessly down through a small metal chute.

Clang! Clone 71 smashed into a metal grille. Crawling aside, he let Clone 11 slam into it.

"Ouch!" yelped Clone 11.

"Man, that had to hurt!" exclaimed Clone 71 as Clone 11 unstuck himself from the grille, grimacing.

"You think?" Clone 11 grimaced again as pain lanced through his body. "We're in the air vents. There has to be a way out of this."

A crash sounded, and they both turned to see RG Clone and the ten soldiers mashed together against the grille. "Hey guys," said a muffled voice from the pile. "We jumped in here after we saw you go down."

"Thanks," said Clone 71. "We needed the company."

The men extricated themselves from the pile and got to their hands and knees.

"Okay, let's go," said Clone 71.

The group crawled through many tunnels. Finally, they came upon the central air unit, which was high enough to walk in.

Everyone lay down to rest except Clone 71. Clone 71 inspected the room. He found nothing of interest except a touch-screen monitor in the corner of the room. He tapped the screen once, and it lit. It showed several options.

"Security systems, cloning rooms, oh there you are," murmured Clone 71. He tapped the security systems option and a new screen appeared. This time, it showed two options. 'Systems' and 'Dispatches'. Clone 71 selected 'Dispatches' and a new screen came up. This time it showed a list of clone soldier dispatches and their locations. He found the air vents.

A bolt of fear struck him. There was a dispatch of thirty clones heading down the tunnel next to the central air unit!

Clone 71 cocked his rifle. "Guys, get all of your grenades. Now."

The men unhooked their grenades.

"On three throw," he called calmly, though he was visibly sweating. "One, two, three!"

They threw their grenades onto the ground. "Jump!" yelled Clone 71 as a huge explosion rocked the central air unit. The floor gave way just as the first of the clones came in.

Boom! All of the upper air vents fell down through the top floor and onto the one below. The enemy clones fell straight down to their deaths, but Clone 71's group jumped into one of the vents.

Their vent hit the ground and ruptured, exposing the shaken, but uninjured men.

Clone 71 got up, dusting himself off.

"We're in."

Chapter 20
Lethal Sewage

Clone 71's group crept through the white halls silently, avoiding the guards and clone soldiers. They were attempting to reach the cloning chamber to observe the security and plan an attack to freeze the cloning process.

Clone 71 peeked into another hallway, but quickly drew back. Three clone guards were walking down the hall towards them!

Clone 71 gripped his blaster rifle hard and prepared to fire as the clones stopped five feet from where he crouched. They looked around for a moment, and then ran to where Clone 71 was.

Smack! Bang! Clunk! The guards went down easily. None of them were conscious now.

Clone 71 wiped some sweat from his face and entered the hall. He looked through the window to his right and saw the cloning chamber. "We are at the chamber. Please stay alert. There are probably many guards here," he announced quietly.

The group nodded as he turned another corner. Suddenly, he found himself on the ground, pinned by a guard. Five others were behind his restrainer.

"One move and your friend dies!" The guard held a long, ugly electro-sword to Clone 71's neck.

The soldiers all dropped their weapons and put their hands on their heads.

Suddenly, RG Clone jumped from his position and tackled Clone 71. They slid across the floor as the electro-sword slashed down.

RG Clone cried out in pain as the sword plunged into his chest. He stayed on the ground as Clone 71 stood up.

"No!" yelled Clone 71. "You'll die for this!"

He gripped his blaster rifle and let loose his anger. The blaster rifle fired off countless shots into RG Clone's killer. The man contorted and flew into the air, hitting the ground hard. He was dead.

A groan was heard behind Clone 71. He turned to face RG Clone, who was now standing. He gripped the sword and pulled it out of his mangled armor.

"Good thing I wore extra chest armor," he said painfully as he showed Clone 71 the hole in his armor. A drop of blood oozed out of a small puncture in his chest.

The clone guards dropped their weapons in awe, and the soldiers pounced silently. A minute later, the guards were sitting against the wall, tied up with wire.

"Great," said Clone 71, clapping his hands. "We'll leave you to it then."

The group marched on towards the cloning chamber, ready for anything.

As Clone 71 walked along, he noticed a pipe ahead. Running up to it, he felt the circumference.

"This is it," said Clone 71 grimly. "We found the sewer pipe.

He took a small electro-sword from his belt and sliced a hole in the pipe. He removed a round marble from a pouch and tapped it three times. The marble transformed into a baseball-sized metal sphere with a small timer on the side. Clone 71 set it for ten minutes and pressed a yellow button on a transmitter hooked to his belt.

The timer began to count down. Clone 71 fed the explosive into the sewer pipe and repaired it.

Suddenly, RG Clone cocked his rifle. "Ten clones. Down the hall. Let's take them!"

Chapter 21
Countdown

RG Clone charged toward the enemy clones and let loose his firepower. They all fell quickly, unable to react to his speed.

Clone 71 and the others ran up to him.

"Nice!" exclaimed Clone 71. "Well done. You really took them out!"

"Freeze!" rapped a voice harshly.

Clone 71 turned to see almost fifty clones pointing weapons at them.

"Drop the weapons!" said the voice again. "Now!"

Clone 71 let his blaster rifle fall to the floor. "They have us good and proper," he announced gravely. "Drop them, men."

Clone 71's team all dropped their weapons hesitantly and put their hands on their heads.

A murmur came from the ranks of clones and they parted to reveal two all too familiar faces.

The Schwartz brothers.

Michael, adorned in black armor, laughed. "They're helpless," he said, drawing a blaster rifle from his belt.

Clone 71 put his hands up as to surrender and let them fall really hard…

Michael gave a strangled yelp and held his sore head. "Brother," he wheezed. "Help me!"

James walked forward and punched Clone 71 in the face, breaking his nose and sending blood everywhere.

RG Clone pushed James Schwartz away. "Leave him alone!" he yelled.

Michael stood up and revealed a small button on his belt. "Shut up or I'll press this button."

Clone 71 shrugged. "So?"

Michael Schwartz chuckled. "What an idiot. This button will kill Clone 13, your buddy who went missing."

RG Clone's knuckles turned white. "How do we get him back?"

James grinned. "You'll die with him. No big deal. We truss you and RG Clone up, send you to be tortured. Then we let you watch you friend, Clone 13, scream and yell as he is tortured. Then, we pull the plug."

Clone 71 laughed insanely. "Well, good for you," he said smugly. "Because this whole place is going to blow up right… NOW!" He dove into an enemy clone as the huge explosion ripped through the facility, cutting it in half.

The Schwartz brothers screamed and ran through their ranks of clones to escape. They soon went out of sight.

Clone 71 picked up his blaster rifle. "I'm going to get Clone 13 out of here!" he called to RG Clone. "Go after the Schwartz twins!"

He ducked as a chunk of ceiling fell down in front of him. He jumped over his obstruction and continued through the collapsing facility towards the dungeon.

Finally, he reached the dungeon. He sprinted into the cell room and…

Nothing. Clone 13 was gone.

Clone 71 screamed and fired his rifle everywhere in his rage.

A yelp was heard, and Clone 71 looked up to see a clone soldier dead in front of him. On his back was a message.

"WE ARE GONE. YOU WON'T FIND THE SCHWARTZ TWINS EVER AND CLONE 13 WILL DIE! FROM YOUR PAL, MICHAEL SCHWARTZ."

Clone 71 sprinted back out of the chamber and found RG Clone. "They escaped. We need to get out of here!" yelled Clone 71.

RG Clone helped Clone 11 up. "There is a way out. There's a ship over there."

Clone 71 looked and saw the clone fighter. It would fit three.

"Hurry!" said Clone 11 as he jumped into the front. "Get in!"

The fighter took off as the clone facility collapsed and gave a final bang as it caved in and was destroyed forever.

Chapter 22
A Strange Finding

Clone 11 piloted the fighter skillfully out of the destroyed structure and flew southeast toward a hill. He set the whining aircraft onto the hill and shut off the engine just before a smoke plume came from the fuel tanks.

"Get out!" screamed Clone 71, diving out of the craft onto the desert sand.

The craft exploded, but Clone 11 and RG Clone flew from the wreckage to land next to him.

They got up and checked their supplies. They had enough ammunition, but sparse food. Their grenades had been lost in the clone facility. The blue bottle that Clone 71 had received was okay, but it was almost gone.

RG Clone squinted into the distance. "Where are they?"

"I don't have a clue," said Clone 11.

Clone 71 scanned the horizon. "Look!" he called out. "There are the mountains!"

"What mountains?" asked Clone 11.

Clone 71 ignored him. "Let's go."

They walked and walked, and finally, they reached the mountains. They had long since left the desert, and they were now very cold.

Clone 71 began to climb the rocks energetically, but the other men were hesitant.

"Come on," Clone 71 coaxed.

The three clones began to climb up the mountain.

After a long, strenuous climb, they reached a flat ledge. They sat there for a while to regain their breath.

"Hey," said Clone 71, panting. "Look over there."

A large gaping hole in the side of the mountain was clearly visible.

"I'm going over there to look at that," said Clone 71. "Watch my back."

Slowly, the clones climbed into the hole.

"Exciting." Clone 11 couldn't contain his sarcasm.

Clone 71 blindly dove through the darkness. "Ouch!" he said.

"We'll wait here," said the other two clones. "Tell us when you get a light."

Clone 71 felt along the wall of this large cave. His foot touched something different than the floor.

Clone 71 bent down and felt the object. It felt like a tent.

He groped for a flap, and he found one. He eased himself into it and his other hand closed around a tube. He flicked the switch upon it and a light blossomed from the flashlight in his grasp.

"Guys," he said strangely. "All this stuff…"

Clone 11 and RG Clone found the flap and entered the large tent. "What the…"

On a small wood box, there was a notebook and a pen. A sniper rifle lay on the floor. There were glossy photos on the ground.

Clone 71 examined the rifle. "This is ancient," he said. "This uses bullets."

He tossed it aside and lifted the notebook away from the box and opened the box. Inside were several papers. He took a yellowed wrinkled one from the bottom and looked at it.

A picture of a handsome young man was glued to the paper, and a small box with writing in it told Clone 71 that the man's name was Sergeant Justin Freeman.

He folded the paper neatly and picked up the largest photo. It showed the same man, only with a smiling little girl and his wife.

A tear coursed down Clone 71's cheek. Wiping it away, he picked up the notebook and opened it.

June 6th, 2010

The first bombs exploded in New York today. I could not find myself as I boarded a plane and left before the radioactive material could get me. I felt like a coward.

June 8th, 2010

The United States is gone. Not a person left there. The nuclear war has devastated China, our attacker, as well. We wiped out over seventy percent of their population, while the other thirty percent is sick and dying.

Because of the fallout, mostly the whole world has been affected. The eastward winds have brought this stuff to the United Kingdom, which is now completely deserted. My family is dead, and I am mourning now.

July 4th, 2010

This was Independence Day. Sadly, I am one of the few people left alive. By few I mean ten or eleven. But one of my friends is a cloner, and he is trying to clone us. This is unsuccessful now though because my friend needs sterilized conditions. We want regular people (clones) like us.

December 1st, 2010

It is hard to write now. I am living in a cave in the Himalaya Mountains. My cloner friend is gone, likely somewhere in the Sahara Desert. He has built a facility called Skyscraper City. The clones look like normal humans! I don't think this is good, but if the human race goes extinct, there is a way to fix the clones back to humans.

Clone 71 finished and put down the book. "Whoa!"

RG Clone was open-mouthed. "I didn't know there was anyone before us."

Clone 71 shook his head. "Yeah, right now, if not for the cloning, we could have families."

There was silence.

"I wonder if the Schwartz brothers know about this," said RG Clone.

Clone 71 nodded. "They probably do, but tried to hide it from us."

"Why would they hide it?" asked Clone 11, confused.

Clone 71 replied, "You couldn't take over the world unless you had a veritable army of obedient robots, like the clones. If you have regular people, they would rebel against you."

"True enough," said Clone 11. "But where…"

A beep interrupted him.

"What?" asked Clone 71.

The beep was louder this time.

Suddenly, a blue light shined from the box. RG Clone reached into the box and pulled out a small PDA.

"Wow!" exclaimed RG Clone. "This is cool!"

Clone 71 peeked at the bright screen. "Go to GPS," he commanded.

RG Clone pressed a button, and a menu came up. The screen read, "One stored location."

"Hit that," murmured Clone 11.

RG Clone pressed another button, and a map came up. It showed…

"Right," said Clone 71. "We're going to the Smithsonian Institute in Philadelphia."

Chapter 23
Philadelphia

The clones read the bottom of the PDA. It said to leave the cave the east way. They did, and they found a helicopter sitting on a rock precariously.

Clone 11 quickly took the pilot's chair, and Clone 71 took the co-pilot's seat. RG Clone hopped into the gunner's chair, and they took off toward the United States.

A day later, they landed on the road next to the Smithsonian Institute.

"Let's go," called Clone 71.

The three clones walked into the building, watching for any movement.

They reached a small map of the building as Clone 71 glanced at the PDA. "It's supposed to be right here," he said, surprised.

RG Clone began to walk away. "What's the point?"

Clone 71, in desperation, called out, "Sergeant Justin Freeman!"

The map melted away in front of his eyes, revealing a small cube with inscriptions in several different languages on it.

"What's this supposed to be?" asked Clone 11.

Clone 71 reached for the cube.

Something slammed into him and propelled him back into a wall. He tried to get up, but a figure dropped from the ceiling to land on him. It was Michael Schwartz.

"How pleasant to see you again," said Michael with hate in his voice. "Perhaps you would like to see my twin as well…"

He outstretched an arm and James Schwartz jumped down as well.

"I got his friend, brother," he said, motioning toward a bound and gagged RG Clone.

"Where's Clone 11?" thought Clone 71 silently.

James turned toward the cube. "What?" he cried out.

It was gone.

Michael turned as well. "How?"

Fiercely, Clone 71 drove his fist into Michael's neck. He fell silently to the floor. James turned and smacked him against the wall. Clone 71 lolled back against the wall, feigning unconsciousness.

James Schwartz would regret turning around…

"Yah!" screamed Clone 11 in his ear as he sliced at James with an electro-sword.

The twin quickly tore off his ruined armor and drew an electro-sword as well. He began to block Clone 11's fierce attacks.

Suddenly, Clone 11 tossed something in the air. "Catch it!" he yelled.

Clone 71 dove and caught the shining cube. Smiling, he untied RG Clone as the two men fought.

"There!" RG Clone cried as he ripped out the gag with his freed arms. "Let's get out of here!"

Clone 11 was busy with James Schwartz, but he heard RG Clone. He swiftly lobbed a sonic grenade at him, and the twin went flying straight into a steel case.

James tumbled to the ground, unconscious.

"All right," said Clone 11. "Let's go."

The clones ran through the doors and took off in their helicopter.

Chapter 24
The Final Briefing

After an hour or so, Clone 11 touched down on a small warehouse roof. The clones got out of the helicopter and sat down to examine the cube.

Clone 71 took it from his pocket. "Sergeant Justin Freeman," he said.

The cube morphed into a small holograph projector. A small silver button blinked on the side. Clone 71 pressed it, and it projected a small model of Florida into the air.

"The place you are looking for is in Florida," said the projector in a monotone. "It is on the tip." The image zoomed in.

RG Clone smiled. "What now?"

"It is an abandoned bunker for the United States military. It was supposed to protect the inhabitants from nuclear attack. The radiation is believed to have overpowered the base, and killed all of the inhabitants." It zoomed in again to show a small building next to the sea.

Clone 71 stood up. "We should be going."

The voice cut off his words. "The only way in is through a small air vent on the floor. Exercise caution inside, for there is a large amount of ammunition in the bunker. If you place a bullet in the wrong place, you could very well blow yourself up."

The projector collapsed and morphed back to a cube form as Clone 71 scooped it up. "All right," he said. "We are going to a building on the Florida coast. There could a billion buildings there."

The cube spoke again. "Downloading to PDA," it said.

The PDA beeped as Clone 71 took it out of his pocket. "There it is!" he cried, pointing to the map that it showed. "Let's get going."

The clones jumped into the helicopter as Clone 11 started the engines. "We're lucky," said Clone 11. "We have enough fuel in this baby to get to where we need to go."

The plane took off slowly, headed for Florida.

After a few hours, they reached the bunker. Clone 11 smoothly touched down a block away from it. "All right," he said. "Let's get out."

The clones jumped out and ran into the bunker, knowing what might happen.

Chapter 25
The Transformation

The clones stormed the building and began to search for the floor vent. The whole place reeked like fish, so they wanted to find it quickly.

Clone 71 scanned the corners of the small room, looking for the vent. He took a step forward and tripped over something.

"Ouch!" cried Clone 71.

RG Clone ran over to him and helped him up. "You okay?" he asked anxiously.

Clone 71 smiled. "Yeah."

Clone 11 ran over as well and pointed at the vent. "You found it by tripping on it, man," he exclaimed.

Clone 71 ripped off the vent and dove into the tunnel. A crash was heard, then silence.

"I think its okay," said RG Clone. He dove in with Clone 11 close behind.

They spilled out of the tunnel onto a hard metal floor. Clone 71 helped them up. "Let's do this!" he yelled out.

They made their way through the dark, winding hallway. Finally, the hall opened up into a huge room occupied by a large fiberglass box that would fit a clone inside comfortably.

"Wow!" exclaimed Clone 71. "Look over there."

A small table was next to the fiberglass chamber. It had a small gadget with three prongs pointing upward. They were only about an inch long apiece.

Clone 71 removed the cube from his pocket and ran toward the strange object. He placed the cube on the prongs. A button appeared on the table. Taking a deep breath, he let his hand fall.

The gadget let loose a small blast of light that made Clone 71 turn briefly. The cube began to levitate and spin rapidly. It was slowly brightening as it spun faster and faster. Suddenly, the light began to pulse outward.

"Look away, guys!" cried Clone 71, a split second before a huge wave of light emanated from the cube and engulfed them.

Then everything turned white.

Inside their bodies, DNA molecules were splitting apart from each other and connecting with different ones. Their features began to change, and their white blood cells killed off any of the cloning chemicals in their bloodstreams. The radiation in their bodies was dispersed and destroyed as well as the radiation outside their bodies. The light traveled through the walls and rippled over the entire planet, destroying the radiation and changing all of the Earth's clones to humans.

Clone 71 smiled. "Alexander Essenes."

"Ryan Hughes," whispered RG Clone.

Clone 11 rolled onto his stomach. "Samuel Steward."

*   *   *   *   *

Confined in a small, freezing cell, Clone 13 whispered, "Jeremy Winters."

Michael Schwartz turned towards him. "What?"

Clone 13's eyes widened a split second before the huge wave of light crashed into him.

Michael growled. "Clone 71!"

James ran into the room. "I have a beacon on the light. It's coming from the bunker."

Michael glanced at Clone 13's body monitor and froze. His heartbeat was…

"Normal! His heartbeat is normal!" he screamed.

James shook his head. "Come on, brother, get him."

Michael destroyed the cuffs on Clone 13's wrists and threw him into the waiting aircraft.

"Get in, filthy scum," he commanded disgustedly.

The plane took off toward the bunker with no further ado.

The cube finally stopped spinning and fell back to the dais as the former clones stood up.

"Wow!" exclaimed Clone 71. "I can't remember my clone number. All I remember for a name is... Alexander Essenes."

Clone 11 smiled. "Me too. I can only remember the name Samuel Steward."

"I'm Ryan Hughes," said RG Clone, looking at their exasperated faces. "It's our human names. But the clone names are on our armor."

Clone 71 gasped. "They're coming. The Schwartz brothers!"

RG Clone could distantly hear clattering down the hallway moving toward the room. "Ready your guns and protect the cube!"

"Why protect the cube?" asked Clone 71 quickly.

RG Clone slapped him. "Read it, smart one!"

Clone 71 grabbed it and read aloud. "Effects can be reversed using this cube," he read. He cried out. "We have to destroy it so the Schwartz brothers can't use it!"

Clone 11 sighed. "Great. Put it in your pocket."

The clattering was very close now.

"Just attack!" yelled RG Clone.

The Schwartz brothers ran in just as the gunfire hit them. They jumped over it just in time and drew their electro-swords. The hail of bolts stopped.

"Let's settle this!" growled James Schwartz.

RG Clone drew three electro-swords and gave one to Clone 71 and Clone 11. They all threw mock salutes. "All right, *Schwartz*," he called. "Let's settle this."

They spread out and encircled them. Then, they fought.

Chapter 26
Underwater

Clone 11 and RG Clone sprang at Michael Schwartz, attempting to take him by surprise, but they lost their advantage when their opponent's sword sprouted another electric end. Clone 71 was charged and nearly stabbed by James before he kicked him away and regained his balance. Slowly, Clone 71 worked up an advantage, forcing James to parry on his weak side. Despite that, James was forcing Clone 71 back with his slightly superior strength. It was plain that Clone 71 was in trouble.

RG Clone sliced at Michael's head and ran into the hallway to escape. It left two-on-two, greatly decreasing the former clones' advantage.

Clone 71 left off James and cannoned into Michael to allow Clone 11 to take the other twin. He gained an advantage quickly because of his sudden attack, and the twin was desperate to fight off his thrusts. In a stroke of desperation, Michael threw a sonic grenade at Clone 71's chest, forcing him high into the air and back to the floor hard. Clone 71 hardly had time to get up before an iron fist slammed into his head and catapulted him to a wall. He began to see double of Michael stabbing down at him…

"Get off of him!" yelled Clone 11, throwing himself against Michael's body and forcing him away, as well as making him drop his sword.

Clone 71's vision cleared and he gripped his opponent's fallen sword. He twirled his two swords. "I'll take you, James!"

James Schwartz raised his sword in an attempt of bravery. "You are…"

Suddenly, a grenade landed next to Clone 71. It exploded and sent him into another wall. Struggling to get up, Clone 71 could see that the grenade was supposed to dull his instincts. He gave up and lay on the floor.

Clone 11 surrendered to Michael and James and put his hands behind his head. "I have no choice," he said.

They were both stunned with another dull grenade and tossed over the Schwartz brothers' backs. "We have you all now."

The twins recovered their swords and ran into the hall. They eventually reached the tunnel. "Up you go," called Michael, pushing Clone 11 up to the floor. James tossed Clone 71 up as well. They followed briskly.

The Schwartz brothers reached the floor and lugged their prisoners into their aircraft. "Nice?" asked James.

"Yeah!" said a voice. "But it is no longer yours."

RG Clone waved from the pilot's chair, smiling. In his hand was a blaster rifle.

The Schwartz brothers responded quickly. James dove at RG Clone and fought for the rifle. Michael streaked into the back of the plane and took a left into a small hallway on the craft. Clone 11 followed, trying to catch him.

Michael grabbed a doorknob and flung in open to reveal a small room. In it was Clone 13, bound with electric cuffs. He looked like he hadn't eaten for months.

Clone 11 reached into his pocket and pulled out a glove. He put it on his hand and took out his blaster rifle. "Do the honors, Mr. Schwartz," he said, his voice shaking.

Michael turned around. "Why of course." He immediately drew a blaster rifle and fired at Clone 11.

The laser bolts flew into the air as Clone 11 jabbed a button on his wrist. A small, glimmering shield of light was projected into the air. The shots hit the shield and bounced everywhere.

Michael stopped shooting. "Very impressive."

Clone 11 smiled. "Not impressive ENOUGH!" He stretched out his gloved hand and yelled, "Give me force!"

The glove began to radiate blue light. Clone 11 closed his hand to hide the light momentarily, and then he opened it.

The light flew through the air and hit Michael in the chest, making him fly into the air and collide with a steel wall. He stood up slowly and fired his blaster rifle three times. All of the shots were perfect, and they hit Clone 11 in the chest.

He was thrown backward into a wall and buckled. Rolling past a fresh volley of shots, he removed his now useless armor and ran back into the room.

Suddenly, an alarm sounded and a metallic voice called, "Approaching five hundred feet."

Clone 11 threw himself at Michael and took his weapon.

"Two hundred feet."

Clone 11 shot at a control panel at the corner of the room and disabled the electric cuffs latching Clone 13 to the wall.

"One hundred feet."

He threw Clone 13 off of the wall and tumbled to the floor. Michael jumped to his feet and scuttled away toward a small red manhole cover on the floor.

"Fifty feet."

Clone 11 ran toward the door, ushering Clone 13 ahead. Michael ripped away the manhole cover and dove into it.

"Ten feet."

Clone 13 tripped and fell before Clone 11 could grab his hand to pull him the rest of the way.

The aircraft plunged into the ocean, throwing Clone 11 into a wall. Clone 13 fell into the open manhole that Michael had gone through.

The door to the room suddenly burst open, and gallons of water cascaded in. Clone 11 was tossed like a doll into the manhole.

There was no oxygen in the small tunnel. It was all water. Clone 11 could see that a small submarine was hooked to the end. "Sly dogs," he thought to himself.

He swam as fast as he could toward the craft. He could see the light in the submarine dimming. He swan faster and faster, and finally he reached the submarine door. He wedged it open and slipped through the space.

Clone 11 found himself in the submarine, safe from drowning in the murky waters. He then lay down on the dark floor and fell asleep, for he was exhausted from the day's labors.

*   *   *   *   *

RG Clone and James jumped from the plane moments before the plane crashed into the sea, grappling with each other in an attempt to get the rifle. James was smacking his opponent in the face to weaken his grip, and RG Clone was using his end of the rifle to smash James Schwartz's kneecaps.

James was unlucky when the pair hit the water because he was on the bottom. He yelled aloud as the skin on his back was ripped to shreds. RG Clone clung to him as he writhed and screamed in pain. Finally, the twin escaped his grasp and plunged underwater. RG Clone followed swiftly.

The water was clear enough for RG Clone to see James and the front of the thing he was swimming toward. He strained forward and nearly gripped James's foot. He growled and sprung forward just as something hit him in the head. He saw stars and everything went black.

Clone 71 was tossed out the window and into the water as the aircraft plunged into the water. Gasping for breath, he looked around for RG Clone. Suddenly, a limp form surfaced next to him. He gripped the body and pounded its chest.

The form coughed up some water and began to tread water.

"Are you okay, Ryan?" he asked.

RG Clone smiled as he coughed again and motioned for Clone 71 to follow him. "Follow me, Alexander."

The two men followed James. After a minute, James submerged and didn't come up again.

"Let's go," said Clone 71.

The two friends dove deep into the water after their enemy. And then they saw the submarine.

RG Clone pointed at a small hatch twenty feet away and Clone 71 nodded. James was nowhere to be seen, but they knew that he was in the submarine.

They swam quickly toward the hatch and pulled it open. RG Clone dove in first, gasping for breath, and Clone 71 shot through like a cannon.

They landed on a cold, hard floor made of a strange tile that felt slippery. Clone 71 got up distastefully, coughing.

"All right," he said. "You need to find Clone 11. I am going to find Clone 13. We'll meet back in this room."

RG Clone got up swiftly and left the room. "Copy that."

Clone 71 removed his blaster rifle from his belt. "I'm going in."

Chapter 27
The Submarine

Clone 71 ducked behind a pillar as footsteps crossed the hall ahead.

"The men aren't ready, James," said Michael Schwartz.

Clone 71 could hear a whisper. Suddenly, a hand pummeled the side of his head, sending him into a wall. He looked up at his attacker. It was Michael Schwartz.

"Hello again, my old friend," he said angrily. "It is so nice to see you." Michael smiled and reached into Clone 71's pocket. He pulled out the cube. "It is so interesting how you kept it so long."

Clone 71 smiled back at him. "I know!" he cried as he drew his blaster rifle and smacked Michael in the side of the head.

Michael dropped the cube onto the ground and lay out flat, whimpering. James attacked Clone 71, but the cube was safe in his pocket again.

Clone 71 retaliated to James's attack and punched James in the side of the head. James reeled and Clone 71 gripped his neck.

"Where is Clone 13?" he growled, aiming the blaster rifle at James, who flinched.

"I don't know," he whimpered. "Michael knows though."

He cowered as Clone 71 moved toward Michael. "And you?"

Michael raised his hands and James socked Clone 71 in the jaw. Clone 71 flew into a wall and slumped to the ground.

"He's done," said Michael Schwartz.

"What did you say?" called Clone 71. He raised his blaster rifle and fired. The shots glanced off of the floor. Slowly, he stood, firing laser bolts galore from his weapon. None of them hit, though.

Clone 71 fired a final shot and ran out of the room with the twins on his tail.

*   *   *   *   *

Clone 11 woke up to many footsteps running toward the room he was in. He pointed his blaster rifle down the hallway.

Suddenly, Clone 71 burst into the room and slammed into the wall. He grinned at Clone 11. "Is there another hall leading from this room?"

Clone 11 grabbed him and sprinted into a different hallway just as the Schwartz brothers dove into the room.

"Where are they?" Michael Schwartz yelled.

"No idea," said James angrily.

In the small hallway, Clone 11 aimed his blaster rifle at James. "What an idiot," he whispered as he fired a lethal shot.

The laser bolt whizzed silently through the air to meet James's shoulder.

The scream that followed was too loud to handle. Clone 71 and Clone 11 streaked away from the scene down a hallway and into a huge room.

It was the control room. The pilot's chair was there as well as many controls. The thing that drew the most eyes was the person strapped to the wall.

It was Clone 13.

"Clone 13," cried Clone 71. He ran toward the emaciated man with his blaster rifle. "How are you?"

Clone 13 could hardly speak. "Awful. I haven't eaten for almost a month."

Clone 71 shot the straps holding his friend and hugged him. "My friend," he called. "You're alive!"

Clone 13 smiled and buried his face into his shoulder. "You saved me," he said softly. "Thank you!"

He moved to Clone 11, who hugged him heartily. "Good to have you back," said Clone 11.

Footsteps were heard, and they whirled around to face the Schwartz brothers, holding a writhing RG Clone.

"Hello my friends," said Michael Schwartz. "I would like to introduce you to my new acquaintance." He drew from his belt a giant electro-sword. It was six feet tall.

Clone 71 shook his head. "You never learn, do you?"

James smiled, despite the wound in his shoulder. "We always learn how stupid you are."

Clone 71's knuckles turned white on his blaster rifle. "Why, I thought you were stupid," he said, moving his blaster rifle so it was aimed at the twins.

Michael swiftly put his electro-sword to RG Clone's throat. "You won't get him," he said, "unless you kill us."

Clone 11 aimed his blaster rifle at the twins as well. "We'll kill you then."

James stepped toward the group. "We could talk this out. Or… you could die."

Clone 71 pretended to debate the possibility. "Yeah, we might die, but you would first."

James removed something from his pocket. It was a small control pad with several buttons on it. The most prominent one was in the center of the device. It said, "SELF-DESTRUCT" on it.

"This controls the submarine," he said. "If you don't agree to our terms, I will press this button." He placed his finger upon the red button.

"All right," called Clone 71. "What are your terms?"

James cleared his throat. "We will give you RG Clone in exchange for the cube," he replied.

Clone 71 drew out the cube. "All right, then," he said. "What are you going to do with it?"

He smiled. "Can't tell you," he said. "Now give it here."

Clone 71 stretched out his hand as James reached for the cube…

Suddenly, Clone 71 whipped forward with his free hand and took the submarine control from James's hand while retaining control of the cube. "I think you should negotiate your terms, Schwartz, for your time is rather short," he said silkily.

James was speechless.

"The cube is going to be destroyed," continued Clone 71 as he pushed on a few controls for the submarine. "I will let it out of the submarine and let the water pressure crush the cube and destroy all of its power."

The large submarine tilted downward and leveled at its lowest possible depth.

Clone 71 pressed another button and a small platform came down from the ceiling. Smiling, he placed the cube onto it. With another press of a button, the platform went back up to the ceiling.

"My friends," said Clone 71. "Please witness the destruction of the cube."

A small window opened on the ceiling, giving all of the men a clear view of the cube as it was released into the waters. Almost instantaneously, the cube was crushed to the size of a piece of paper. Then, the flattened cube fell apart into little pieces the size of a grain of sand and disappeared, never to be seen again.

Michael was very angry. "I'll kill RG Clone now, then," he said. He whirled back with his electro-sword and slashed off the helpless man's arm.

RG Clone screamed and fell to the floor in agony as Michael laughed. He kept laughing until he saw the look…

Anger, revenge, hate, and sadness were etched upon the Clone 71's face as he charged toward Michael Schwartz with nothing more than his blaster rifle. He bowled past James and brought his blaster rifle down onto his victim's head, who was thrown down to the floor.

Stunned, Michael dropped his electro-sword. Clone 71 took advantage of the brief pause to pummel Michael three more times with the rifle. The twin cried out in pain and kicked Clone 71 in the leg, forcing it back and making the ex-clone fall. Michael got up quickly with his electro-sword in hand and sliced down at the man.

Suddenly, something slammed into Michael and threw him to the floor. Clone 71 got up slowly and turned to face Michael, who had beaten him up. He was holding his electro-sword next to his neck. Clone 71 could feel his hairs prickling with the electricity.

"Time to die," said Michael as he brought the sword back for the stab.

Almost in slow motion, a figure dove in between the two with an electro-sword and stabbed into the twin's chest just before Michael's sword pierced his own chest.

The figure tumbled to the ground as Michael stood, staring at Clone 71. Slowly, ever so slowly, he went to his knees and tipped over onto his side, dead.

Clone 71 ran to his rescuer's side and knelt next to him. "Are you all right?" he asked softly.

The man turned his face toward Clone 71 slowly. "When I saw what my twin was going to do," said James Schwartz. "I thought for a moment that your life and the mankind were more important than me."

Clone 71 caught his breath. "You," he stuttered, "saved…my life?"

James smiled weakly. "I guess I did."

The ex-clone chuckled as he unbuckled James's armor. "I better check your wound," he said.

"The heck with that," said the cloner. "I'm going to die anyway. But before I go, I need to tell you our secret."

Clone 71 looked at the pale face. "What secret?" he asked.

James Schwartz smiled again. "Let me tell you."

Chapter 28

The Schwartz Legacy

"Michael and I were born to a chemist and a scientist. We were very wealthy, so we were able to go to a five star scientific college."

"When we were about ten years old, we were capable of building high-grade nuclear weapons. So, we traveled to China, who requested our services."

"In China, we made nuclear weapons. But Michael wanted more. After working for ten years, Michael broke into the control room and sent six nuclear bombs to the United States. The whole country was destroyed by radiation. However, some retaliation bombs from the United States hit China. We tracked them and left in a super-sonic jet before they destroyed the whole place."

"Oh no, Michael wasn't done. He lured me into it and made me create a remote access link to the United States control room and launch missiles everywhere. I did, and the whole world was wiped out except our new cloning facility and Skyscraper City."

"We thought that all humankind was gone. Until a clone scout ventured through the Himalayas and found the US army soldier named Sergeant Justin Freeman. Michael killed him straightaway, but I luckily obtained DNA samples and hid them in the cube, which was in the man's backpack. Those samples could be activated to bring mankind back."

"Eventually, Michael wormed the location out of me and moved it to the Smithsonian Institute in Philadelphia. It was just before you escaped the facility the first time, so he thought it was perfectly safe. Even when you escaped, he thought you wouldn't find out."

"Of course, you live and learn. Michael did his share of learning from you. He learned how smart you were, how hardy you were, and how much you could pick up. When he lost track of you in the Himalayas, he still didn't think that you would find that cave. You did, and with that finding you found out about the cube. The PDA that was in there was mine. I planted it there so you could find it. I knew you would find it, no doubt about that."

"When you found the cube at the Smithsonian Institute, Michael was in a rage. If he had known that I had downloaded the audio files to tell you where to go, I would have been killed. He also said I couldn't do anything right."

"I began to doubt him. I began to hate him. He became my enemy and you became my friend. I tried to help you any way I could without my brother noticing. When the power of the cube was released, I was happy. But we still had Clone 13."

"I knew you would find a way onto the submarine, so I placed Clone 13 onto the wall of the main room. I told Michael that it was for jeering purposes. While we were talking, he saw you and tried to kill you. I jumped into combat and tried to as well. I wasn't completely turned toward you yet."

"When you shot me, I yelled in pain, forcing my brother to take care of me briefly, buying you more time. You left and ran into the room."

James sighed.

"Then the battle happened. The negotiations happened. Finally, I saw Michael for who he truly was. He was a horrible person, seeking only to destroy, not to rebuild. After he cut RG Clone's arm off, I saw everything. The plot to destroy the world. Why he did it. It was all for his gain. So, I made the leap, and here we are."

He smiled as RG Clone slid across the floor to lie next to him. "Well," James said. "I am done here."

James Schwartz took his final breath and his eyes closed gently for the last time.

Chapter 29
A Growing Society

July 4th, 2050

I am writing on my electronic diary as I look out from the five hundredth floor of the Pavilion, the skyscraper in the center of a glittering New York City. I have greatly loved New York ever since it was colonized, and now I live there. Today is the anniversary of James Schwartz, the courageous man who is the real reason for the existence of humanity. I watch as the fireworks burst in the sky and I wonder what would have happened if James hadn't died. He was my enemy until the final moments of his life, when he was my brother. I am grateful for his sacrifice. He was a very brave man indeed.

Humanity is thriving, much to my relief. The world has a total population of one million people, and growing fast. I hope that this will continue for a long time.

My blaster rifle is now hung on the wall in memory of those days of loss and sacrifice. I hope that it will never happen again. I do not want to go through losing friends again. It is too much.

As this day ends, I want to remember all of my friends that I have lost, all the things I have done. I want to hang up my sword forever, but it isn't a guarantee that nothing will happen to this world to place it in danger again.

May peace be to Earth and all of its inhabitants.

With passion,

Alexander Essenes

About the Author

Matthew Reade is a young author who lives in Northern California with his family. He is an avid reader; he enjoys reading fantasy, science fiction, and historical fiction books. His hobbies include reading, writing, playing videogames, and golfing.

www.ingramcontent.com/pod-product-compliance
Lightning Source LLC
Chambersburg PA
CBHW080748250626
47162CB00010B/3062